CW01021707

About the Book

Nobody understood why Billy Harper and his father bought the dumpy old automobile on the used-car lot. It was old-fashioned and its paint had faded. Its windows were broken and it looked like a pile of junk. What the Harpers did with the old car, however, showed their friends that old things can become useful and valuable and can be a source of pleasure for someone who cares about them.

For antique car buffs, Joan Drescher's warm and light-hearted drawings duplicate in precise detail particular features of the Model A.

1930 TOWN SEDAN

1930 CABRIOLET

1929 MAIL DELIVERY

1929 POPCORN WAGON

1930 STANDARD COUPE

1928 FORD OPEN PICKUP

OTHER BOOKS BY THE AUTHOR

An American Revolutionary War Reader
A Civil War Sampler
The Double Quest
The First Book of the Barbarian Invaders
The First Book of Medieval Man
Greta the Strong
Lock, Stock, and Barrel
The Lost Dispatch
Secret Agents Four
Stocks and Bonds (with Rose Sobol)
The Strongest Man in the World
Two Flags Flying
Two-Minute Mysteries
The Wright Brothers at Kitty Hawk

ENCYCLOPEDIA BROWN BOOKS

Encyclopedia Brown and the Case of the Secret Pitch
Encyclopedia Brown, Boy Detective
Encyclopedia Brown Finds the Clues
Encyclopedia Brown Gets His Man
Encyclopedia Brown Keeps the Peace
Encyclopedia Brown Saves the Day
Encyclopedia Brown Solves Them All

MILTON, THE MODEL A

DONALD J. SOBOL

Illustrated by
Joan E. Drescher

HARVEY HOUSE, INC.
PUBLISHERS
IRVINGTON-ON-HUDSON, NEW YORK

Second Printing

Text Copyright © 1971 by Donald J. Sobol. Illustrations Copyright © 1971 by Joan E. Drescher. All rights reserved, including the right to reproduce this book or portions thereof in any form. Library of Congress Catalog Card Number 70-159977. Printed in USA.

*For Aunt Bess
and
Uncle Ben Trencher*

The little Model A stood in a corner of the used-car lot.

Its paint had faded. Its horn did not blow. Its windows were cracked and broken.

Around it were other old cars. But none was so old as the little Model A.

Some of the cars looked like others on the lot, or like those going by on Main Street.

But none looked like the Model A.

In snow and in rain the little Model A stood in the corner. It was too old, too worn-out. And it looked so different from every other car.

Nobody wanted it. Or so it seemed.

Then Mr. and Mrs. Harper and their son Billy moved to town. The day after they had unpacked, Billy and his father stopped at the used-car lot.

They didn't bother to look at any of the new used cars. They went straight up to the Model A.

They walked slowly around the car, twice.

Billy looked underneath it.

"Not much rust, Dad," he said.

"It isn't missing many parts," said his father.

"You could paint it red, and have a nice, smart, little car," the used-car man said. "Right now," he added quickly, "it doesn't run. So I'll let you have it cheap."

"All right," said Billy's father. "You've made a sale."

He paid the used-car man. Then he hooked the little Model A behind his station wagon and pulled the old car home.

Billy's mother put her hands on her hips when she saw the Model A in the driveway.

"You finally found one!" she exclaimed.

Although she shook her head, Billy's mother really wasn't angry. She just didn't know what to make of such an old wreck.

The neighbors were puzzled, too. They crowded around the Model A. They knocked the fenders and kicked the thin tires.

They talked about what a wonderful car it had been in its day.

Of course they really didn't understand why anyone would *buy* such an old car. Mr. Harper ran a bank. He could buy a big, shiny new car.

What were the Harpers going to do
with such a pile of junk?
Indeed, what *could* be done with it?

18

19

Billy and his father knew.

Billy got a hose and washed off the dirt. Then he helped his father to push the old car into the garage.

Mr. Harper closed the door and locked it, leaving the neighbors to wonder harder than ever.

As the weeks passed, the Harpers' station wagon stood outside in the rain and snow. The Model A was kept hidden inside the warm garage.

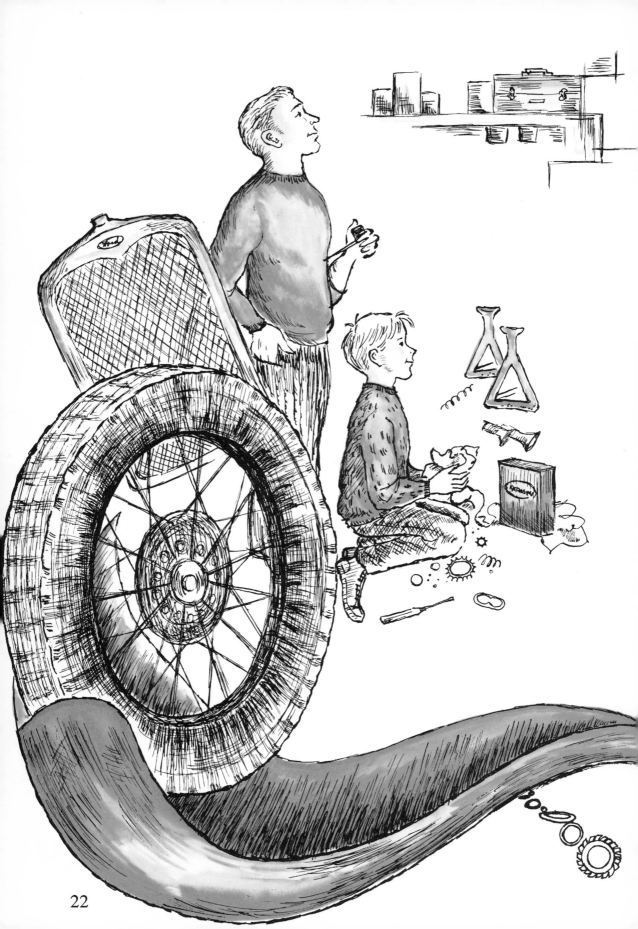

Billy and his father were taking the old car apart, piece by piece!

Mr. Harper worked every evening on the car.

Billy worked on it on weekends and holidays. He scraped each piece and washed it in kerosene.

As each part came off, it was marked and put into a box. Billy's father wanted to be sure to get everything back together.

The work of taking apart, cleaning, and marking went on for many weeks. At last, the bare frame stood on four blocks in the center of the garage.

Billy and his father placed the large parts against the walls. But there was still not enough room to work.

So Billy moved his bicycle onto the porch. Then he helped his father carry twelve boxes filled with the small parts down to the basement.

That was the evening his father smiled and said, "We're ready to start putting the old fellow together!"

He hung a calendar on the garage wall above the fenders. With a red crayon he circled July 3.

"We have only seven months," he said.

"We can do it, Dad," said Billy. He stared at the date, July 3. That date seemed more important than his own birthday.

JULY

SUN	MON	TUE	WED	THU	FRI	SAT
				1	2	3

Every day after that Billy's mother watched the postman bring new parts for the Model A.

"I might as well join the fun," she said. "Otherwise, I'll never get to see you two."

So she sent away for twenty yards of brown mohair. She began to make new upholstery.

As each day passed, Mr. Harper crossed it off his calendar. Suddenly, there was only one day left before July 3.

Mr. Harper came home early from the bank. He and Billy went straight into the garage. Mrs. Harper brought their dinner to them there.

Night fell, and too soon Billy had to go to bed. He lay awake a long time, excited and worried. Finally, he fell asleep to the sound of his father putting on the bumpers.

In the morning his mother woke him. Billy saw that she was beaming. The Model A was done and ready to roll!

When the rest of the neighborhood was first climbing out of bed, Mr. Harper opened the garage door. He got behind the flat, black steering wheel. Billy sat beside him. Mrs. Harper sat in back.

Mr. Harper pressed his foot on the starter and pulled out the choke. The motor missed. Billy held his breath.

"Please . . ." he thought. "Please . . ."

His father tried again. The motor coughed—and turned over. Silky power shot through the new wires and the new fuel line. The little motor hummed.

Mr. Harper said, "Let's go, Milton," for that was the name Billy had chosen.

28

Mr. Harper pushed the button in the middle of the steering wheel. *Ahooga*, sounded the horn. *Ahooga!*

Out of the garage rolled the Model A—old no longer!

Sunlight danced over the freshly painted black fenders and the maroon body. The bright metal of the headlights and the bumpers flashed and sparkled.

Billy sat up straight and proud as they drove through town. They turned off Main Street and onto the highway.

"I hope we get there in time," he said.

His father pressed down on the gas pedal, and Milton seemed to leap forward joyfully.

Shortly before twelve o'clock Mr. Harper turned off the highway and drove to a large field. In the center of the field stood a banner with the words: NATIONAL MODEL A CLUB.

On the field were two hundred gleaming Model A's standing in a circle. Some had come more than two thousand miles to reach the car meet. Like Milton, they all looked brand new.

Some were closed cars, and some were sporty roadsters, phaetons, and cabriolets. Some had two doors, and some had four doors. Some were station wagons. Some were trucks. There were even a taxicab and a school bus.

National Model A Club

School Coach

Billy's father was shown where to park in the big circle. Soon people were hurrying over to Milton.

Many of the men wore straw hats and knickers. Many of the women wore old-fashioned dresses and shoes.

The men did not kick the thin tires.

They did not knock the fenders.

Nobody said what a wonderful car Milton was.

They said what a wonderful car Milton *is*.

"Glad you got here in time for the judging," the head judge said to Billy.

"Do you think Milton will win a prize, Dad?" whispered Billy.

"I hope so," replied his father. "But let's not count on winning anything."

Billy watched the judges. They were looking over, under, and around a yellow roadster. After several minutes they moved on to the next car in the big circle.

Billy looked at the other cars in Milton's class—1930-1931 closed Model A's. He thought Milton was easily the most beautiful of all of them.

Then he saw the blue car.

It was just like Milton, except that Milton's spare tire was in the back. The blue car had *two* spare tires, one in each front fender. And on each spare tire was a gleaming mirror.

"I'll bet Milton could make it eat dust in a race," thought Billy.

When it came Milton's turn to be judged, Billy's father got into the car.

He started the engine, sounded the "ahooga" horn, and turned on the windshield wiper and the lights. Everything worked perfectly.

Billy was so nervous that he couldn't look. But he made himself watch the judging of the blue car. Everything on it worked perfectly, too.

Billy glanced back at Milton. The single spare tire in the rear looked so plain and so lonely.

"I wish the used-car man could see Milton now!" Billy thought, trying to forget the blue car with its two spare tires and two gleaming mirrors.

At six o'clock the prizes were given out. There was a first, a second, and a third prize for each of the seven classes of cars.

At last Milton's class was announced.

The head judge held up a large silver trophy. He looked at Billy. Then he looked at the owner of the blue car.

"The contest was very close," he said. "But first prize goes to the town sedan owned and restored by Mr. and Mrs. Harper and their son, Billy!"

"Go up and get it," whispered Billy's father.

Billy was so scared that he could hardly move his feet. He shook hands with the head judge and clutched the trophy.

His mother put the trophy beside her on the back seat. During the trip home Billy kept turning around to make sure it was really there.

Nothing, he thought, could make him happier.

Mr. Harper turned off the highway and drove through town.

A man in a big new car pulled alongside and shouted, "You've got a little beauty! Want to trade?"

"No, thank you," said Mr. Harper.

They drove down Main Street and stopped at the red light by the used-car lot. And that was the happiest moment of all.

For the used-car man ran onto the sidewalk. He waved his arms.

"Wait! Wait!" he screamed. "Will you sell me your little car?"

"No, thank you!" called Mr. Harper and Billy together.

The light changed from red to green. Mr. Harper shifted gears. Milton sped smoothly for home, singing out, *Ahooga! Ahooga!*

1930 TOWN SEDAN

1930 CABRIOLET

1929 MAIL DELIVERY

1929 POPCORN WAGON

1930 STANDARD COUPE

1928 FORD OPEN PICKUP

About the Author

Don Sobol's many books for young people are known throughout the juvenile book world. Less known, perhaps, is his penchant for antique cars — particularly Model A's. For the past nine years, he has daily driven a car exactly like MILTON, THE MODEL A. He and his wife and their four children make their home in Miami, Florida.

About the Artist

Illustrating children's books was a dream of Joan Drescher's even when she was a little girl. Born to parents who were both artists, she studied at the Rochester Institute of Technology, Parsons School of Design and at the Art Students League. Her work has been exhibited at art shows and in galleries, and she has illustrated several children's books. Mrs. Drescher and her husband, Kenneth, live with their three children in a century-old farmhouse in Hingham, Mass.